Gg

Hh

Ii

Jj

Kk

Ll

Mm

Uu

Vv

Ww

Xx

Yy

Zz

Dear Parent,

The My First Steps to Reading® series is based on a teaching activity that helps children learn to recognize letters and their sounds. The use of predictable language patterns and repetition of familiar words will also help your child build a basic sight vocabulary. Your child will enjoy watching the characters in the books place imaginative objects in "letter boxes." You and your child can even create and fill your own letter box, using stuffed animals, cut-out pictures, or other objects beginning with the same letter. The things you can do together are limited only by your imagination. Learning letters will be fun—the first important step on the road to reading.

The Editors

My "q" Book

(The letter "q" has no sound of its own and is always followed by the letter "u," which does not work as a vowel when used in this way.)

written by Jane Belk Moncure

illustrated by Colin King

Little  had a box.

"I will find things that begin
with the letter 'q,' " she said.

"I will put them into my sound box."

Little

found quilts . . .

quite a lot of quilts.

Two quails watched her quietly.

Little q folded the quilts

and filled her box with quilts.

There was one quilt left.

Little  wrapped the quilt around herself.

"I can be a queen," she said.

Just then, Little  met a real queen.

"If you want to look like a real queen, you must have a crown," said the queen.

So Little  decided to buy a crown.

Little q went to a shop.

Little  bought a crown.

The two queens played until
they were hungry.

Little  went back to the shop.

She bought
some quinces

and some  quince jam.

Then she and the queen ate lunch.

Little q put what

was left into the box.

Then Little q said, "It's late!

Let's go to bed."

"No! No!" said the queen.

"A real queen must have a queen's bed."

Little  was quite sad.

She had no more money. Now she could not buy a queen's bed.

Then Little  saw her box with all the quilts inside.

"I will turn my box into a queen's bed," she said.

Little  put a quilt
on top of the box.

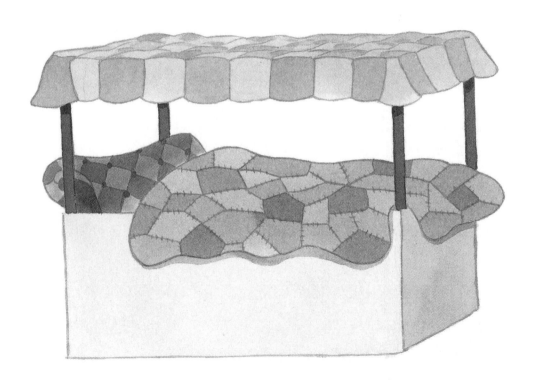

"Now let's go to bed," she said.
She jumped into the box.

"No! No! No!" said the real queen.

So they began to quarrel . . .

until  quarter past nine.

By then, the real queen
was so tired she quit.

So she jumped
into the box with Little .
They pulled up the
quilts and went to sleep.

Can you read these words with Little  ?

quartet

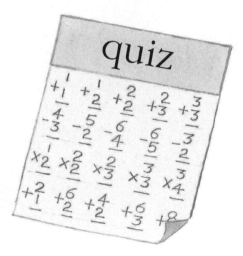

quiz

question mark

"quotation marks"

quills

quince

quintuplets

quail

Aa Bb Cc Dd Ee Ff

Nn Oo Pp Qq Rr Ss Tt

My First Steps to READING®